SANTA COW STUDIOS

SANTA COW STUDIOS

BY
Cooper Edens

ILLUSTRATED BY
Daniel Lane

SIMON & SCHUSTER
BOOKS FOR
YOUNG READERS

To James Earl Jersey

— C. E.

To Alec Guernsey

— D. L.

SIMON & SCHUSTER BOOKS FOR YOUNG READERS
An imprint of Simon & Schuster Children's Publishing Division
1230 Avenue of the Americas, New York, NY 10020
Text copyright © 1995 by Cooper Edens. Illustrations copyright © 1995 by Daniel Lane.
All rights reserved including the right of reproduction in whole or in part in any form.
Simon & Schuster Books for Young Readers is a trademark of Simon & Schuster.
Designed by Paul Zakris. The text of this book is set in 14-point Futura Bold.
The illustrations were done in watercolor accompanied by color pencil.
Manufactured in the United States of America.
10 9 8 7 6 5 4 3 2 1

Library of Congress Cataloging-in-Publication Data
Edens, Cooper.
Santa Cow Studios / by Cooper Edens ; illustrated by Daniel Lane.
p.   cm.
Summary: On a boring New Year's Day, the Santa Cows whisk the
Schwartz family away on a tour of the Santa Cow Movie Studio, complete
with screenings of such films as "Cowsablanca" and "It's an Udderful Life."
[1. Cows—Fiction. 2. Motion pictures—Fiction. 3. Stories in rhyme.]
I. Lane, Daniel, ill.   II. Title.
PZ8.3.E21295Sam   1995   [E]—dc20   94-38666
ISBN: 0-689-80030-4

After a Christmas Eve surprise and a Cow Island New Year's vacation, let us rejoin the Schwartzes and their faithful guides the Santa Cows as they continue their frolicking holiday excursion....

'Twas New Year's Day morning, all my children were bored,
So I said to the Santa Cows, "I need them restored!"
"'Tis our pleasure," the Cows mooed. "Let's leave right away,
For a Santa Cow Studios tour in groovin' L.A."

It took only seconds for all of us to pack,
To cram our rare seashells into every knapsack.
It was lucky El Niño blew all afternoon.
But how could it be that we landed on the moon?

We realized soon after, we were in a studio.
"Shhh," whispered the Angus, "we're taping a video,
A historical one, but we'll show you what's HOT,
We'll show you all the flicks being shot on our lot."

"Here's a great epic being filmed before you now,
Our most lavish production since *Citizen Cow*;
Starring Charlton Holstein as *Moo-ses* the prophet,
It's *The Ten Cowmandments*—nothing will top it!"

"And now," said the Jersey from her lofty sound boom,
"The Guernsey will seat you in our plush screening room.
Rest on rich Naugahyde as you watch the preview...
Of *Star Cows, Cowsablanca,* and *Jurassic Cows, too.*"

"I've been waiting for you, Obi Wan Cow-nobi.
We meet again at last. The circle is now complete.
When I left you I was but a learner. Now I am the master."
"Only a master of evil, Darth Udder."

"Of all the salt licks in all the world, she had to walk into mine. If she can take it . . . I can. Play it again, Bossy."

"Are you crazy? That's a Jurassic Cow.
You think you can control a beast like that?
Cows and Jurassic Cows aren't supposed
to live together."

"How are you Schwartzes enjoying the 'Cowzation'?
We think it adds a lot to each presentation.
Though to some it offends and breaks ethics and vows,
Look what magic it brings to *The Wizard of Cows!*"

"This way," said the Ayrshire, "to our special project,
A great picture that should earn us lasting respect;
We have cast parts for children, for husband and wife...
So watch for your cues in *It's an Udderful Life.*"

'Twas my Elwood who got the first of our stage calls,
And delivered his lines, "Hello, Hereford Falls!
Merry Christmas, you wonderful old Seed & Feed!
Merry Christmas, D. Q.! Merry Christmas indeed!"

On rode Elwood (as George) to his kids joyfully;
I arrived (playing Mary); we hugged tearfully.
"Everyone downstairs quick," I spoke up right on cue,
"The Santa Cows are here, a miracle's come true!"

The final scene was shot beside a Christmas tree,
Starring Schwartzes and our extended family.
Our son Dex offered a toast to all gathered round:
"To my mom and dad, the coolest couple in town!"

Then, as the cowbells on the tree swung to and fro,
Dot, our youngest daughter, all but stole the show.
"Look, Daddy. Teacher says every time a bell rings,
A Santa Cow somewhere gets white angel wings!"

So learn from us Schwartzes, enjoy life's ice creams
And reality will be as sweet as your dreams.